The 39 Steps, Abridged

Adapted by
Patrick Barlow

From the novel by
John Buchan

From the movie by Alfred Hitchcock

Licensed by ITV Global Entertainment Limited

And an original concept by Simon Corble
and Nobby Dimon

ISBN 978-0-573-70958-6

www.concordtheatricals.com
www.concordtheatricals.co.uk
Cover Illustration by Mark Thomas

the producer and/or presenter of such performances to civil penalties. Both amateurs and professionals considering a production are strongly advised to apply to the appropriate agent before starting rehearsals, advertising, or booking a theatre. A licensing fee must be paid whether the title(s) is presented for charity or gain and whether or not admission is charged. Professional/Stock licensing fees are quoted upon application to Concord Theatricals Corp.

This work is published by Samuel French, an imprint of Concord Theatricals Corp.

No one shall make any changes in this title(s) for the purpose of production. No part of this book may be reproduced, stored in a retrieval system, scanned, uploaded, or transmitted in any form, by any means, now known or yet to be invented, including mechanical, electronic, digital, photocopying, recording, videotaping, or otherwise, without the prior written permission of the publisher. No one shall share this title(s), or any part of this title(s), through any social media or file hosting websites.

For all inquiries regarding motion picture, television, online/digital and other media rights, please contact Concord Theatricals Corp.

MUSIC AND THIRD-PARTY MATERIALS USE NOTE

Licensees are solely responsible for obtaining formal written permission from copyright owners to use copyrighted music and/or other copyrighted third-party materials (e.g., artworks, logos) in the performance of this play and are strongly cautioned to do so. If no such permission is obtained by the licensee, then the licensee must use only original music and materials that the licensee owns and controls. Licensees are solely responsible and liable for clearances of all third-party copyrighted materials, including without limitation music, and shall indemnify the copyright owners of the play(s) and their licensing agent, Concord Theatricals Corp., against any costs, expenses, losses and liabilities arising from the use of such copyrighted third-party materials by licensees. For music, please contact the appropriate music licensing authority in your territory for the rights to any incidental music.

IMPORTANT BILLING AND CREDIT REQUIREMENTS

If you have obtained performance rights to this title, please refer to your licensing agreement for important billing and credit requirements.

All producers of *The 39 Steps, Abridged* must give credit to the Author of the Play in all programmes distributed in connection with performances of the Play, and in all instances in which the title of the Play appears for the purposes of advertising, publicizing or otherwise exploiting the Play and/or a production. The name of the Author must appear on a separate line on which no other name appears, immediately following the title and must appear in size of type not less than fifty per cent of the size of the title type.

In addition the following credit must be given in all programmes and publicity information distributed in association with this piece:

THE 39 STEPS, ABRIDGED

Adapted by Patrick Barlow

From the novel by John Buchan

From the movie by Alfred Hitchcock,

licensed by ITV Global Entertainment Limited

And an original concept by Simon Corble and Nobby Dimon

FIREARMS AND OTHER WEAPONS USED IN THEATRE PRODUCTIONS

With regards to the rules and regulations of firearms and other weapons used in theatre productions, we recommend that you read the Entertainment Information Sheet No. 20 (Health and Safety Executive). This information sheet is one of a series produced in consultation with the Joint Advisory Committee for Broadcasting and the Performing Arts. It gives guidance on the management of weapons that are part of a production, including fi rearms, replicas and deactivated weapons.

This sheet may be downloaded from: www.hse.gov.uk.

CHARACTERS

RICHARD HANNAY
COMPERE
MR MEMORY
ANNABELLA SCHMIDT
HEAVY 1
HEAVY 2
BUSINESS MAN 1
BUSINESS MAN 2
PAPERBOY
PORTER
POLICEMAN 1
POLICEMAN 2
VOICES
PAMELA EDWARDS
RADIO ANNOUNCER
LOUISA JORDAN
PROFESSOR JORDAN
SHERIFF
MR DUNWOODY
MR MCQUARRIE
MRS MCGARRIGLE
MR MCGARRIGLE
SUPERINTENDANT ALBRIGHT

SETTING

London, Edinburgh and the Scottish Highlands

TIME

1935

AUTHOR'S NOTE

The 39 Steps, Abridged is the 60 minute (approx.) version of my play *The 39 Steps*.

It is written for four actors.

HANNAY is played by one man throughout.

The woman plays **ANNABELLA** and **PAMELA**.

The other two actors , the **CLOWNS,** play all the other parts. They can be two men, two women or a man and a woman.

NB It is possible (and I have seen it done) – to cast the play with a company of at least fifty. A bit more expensive but jolly good fun.

STYLE OF PLAYING

This is not a naturalistic play.

That should be born in mind throughout. It should be played in the rapid, clipped and heightened style of 1930s thrillers.

SPEED and CLARITY are of the essence.

There should be no pauses in the dialogue apart from when it says PAUSE ie those moments of the most essential DRAMATIC nature.

The Professor raises his little finger. "Are you sure it wasn't – PAUSE – this one?!"

This is essential.

Finally, the more the audience is several steps behind the better.

Do not wait for them.

They'll catch up.

They'll thank you for it.

Overture

(The company run on. Furiously pull on the set for Scene One. They bow and exit. [NB Perhaps funnier if it is just the CLOWNS *who do all scene shifting].)*

Hannay's Apartment. London. Night.

(Various ladders, sheets, paint pots. A large armchair. A window with a blind. Sitting in the armchair is **RICHARD HANNAY**. *Pipe between his teeth.)*

HANNAY. London. Nineteen thirty-five. August. Hannay's the name. Richard Hannay. Thirty-seven. Sound in wind and limb. Twenty years serving the old country, couple of medals, thanks very much, good luck old chap and back home. Which is no home at all if you want to know. Just a dull little rented flat in West One. Portland Place actually. So here I am. All alone and bored. No, more than bored. Tired. Tired of the world and tired of – life to be honest. Wars, elections, more elections, more wars. And who the bloody hell cares frankly? What happens to the world. What happens to people. What happens to me. No-one'd miss me. I wouldn't miss me. I could quite easily just open that window and –

(Moves to window and stops sharply.)

Wait a minute! What the hell are you talking about Hannay! Don't end it all now! *DO something you bloody fool!!!* Something mindless and trivial. Something utterly pointless. Something – I know! A WEST END SHOW!

(Leaps up.)

That should do the trick!

(Marches off.)

MUSIC: ["MR MEMORY THEME"]

Music Hall. London. Night.

(**COMPERE** *and* **MR MEMORY** *enter. Tailcoats and dicky bows. They bow.*)

COMPERE. Good evenin' ladies and gentlemen. I now have the 'onour and prilevege to presentin' to you one of the most remarkable men ever in the whole world. Mr Memory!

(**MR MEMORY** *bows.*)

(*Sound effects: Applause.*)

Every day Mr Memory commits to memory fifty new facts and remembers every one of them. In fact more facts is in his brain than is possible to conceive! Now then, are you ready for the questions Mr Memory?

MEMORY. Quite ready thankoo. I shall now place my inner bein' in a state of mental readiness for this evenin's performance. Thankoo.

(**MEMORY** *enters a trance-like state.*)

MUSIC: ["DRUMROLL"]

(**HANNAY** *appears in a theatre box.*)

COMPERE. Now then ladies and gents. First question please?

(*A woman slips into the next seat to* **HANNAY.** *She peers through opera glasses. Her name is* **ANNABELLA SCHMIDT.** *We imagine the audience shout out questions.*)

Beg pardon sir? Who won the Cup in 1926, Mr Memory?

MEMORY. Who won the Cup in 1926? The Tottenham Hotspurs won the cup in nineteen twenty-six, defeatin' the Arsenal Gunners by five goals to nil. Am I right sir?

COMPERE. Quite right, Mr Memory!

(*Sound effects: Applause.*)

Next question please! What was that sir? What was Napoleon's horse called?

MEMORY. Napoleon's horse was called Bellerophon what he rode at the Battle of Waterloo, June the fifteenth, eighteen fifteen. Am I right sir?

COMPERE. Quite right, Mr Memory!!

(*Sound effects: Applause.*)

(**HANNAY** *jumps up.* **ANNABELLA** *looks shocked.*)

HANNAY. How far is Winnipeg from Montreal?

MEMORY. Distance from Winnipeg to Montreal? One thousand four hundred and fifty three miles. Am I right sir?

HANNAY. Quite right.

(*Sound effects: Applause.*)

COMPERE. Next question please?

(**ANNABELLA** *spots something.*)

ANNABELLA. (*Looks into audience.*) Sheisse!

(*She pulls out a gun. Fires into the air.* **MEMORY** *freezes in shock.*)

(*Sound effects: Audience Pandemonium.*)

COMPERE. Calm down, ladies and gents! Calm down PLEASE!

HANNAY. Did you hear that!!?

ANNABELLA. Excuse me?

HANNAY. Yes?

ANNABELLA. May I come home viz you?

HANNAY. It's a little tricky at the moment. I've got the decorators in and –

ANNABELLA. *PLEASE! You have to!*

HANNAY. Well, it's your funeral!

(They run out. **MR MEMORY** *still in shock.)*

MEMORY. How far's Winnipeg from Napoleon? Who won the Cup in Belleraphon? Nineteen Tottenham Hotspurs! Thankoo thankoo!!!

COMPERE. Thank you Mr Memory.

MEMORY. Thankoo thankoo!!!

COMPERE. Off man, off!

(Shoves him off. Shouts into orchestra pit.)

Play man, play!!

MUSIC: ["MR MEMORY THEME"]

(Sound effects: Applause.)

Hannay's Apartment. London. Night.

(Ladders, paint pots, sheets. A table with telephone. A window with a blind.)

(HANNAY and ANNABELLA enter.)

HANNAY. Some light I think.

ANNABELLA. Wait!

(She runs to the window. Peers through. Pulls the blind.)

Now!

(HANNAY pulls the light switch.)

(Lights up.)

So Richard Hannay.

HANNAY. How do you know my name?

ANNABELLA. I saw it in the lobby.

HANNAY. Ah yes. So may I know your name?

ANNABELLA. Schmidt. Annabella Schmidt.

HANNAY. Well Annabella Schmidt, it was you who fired that shot in the theatre wasn't it? It wasn't a great show but it wasn't that bad.

ANNABELLA. It was a diversion. There were two men in the theatre trying to shoot me.

HANNAY. It sounds like a spy story.

ANNABELLA. That's exactly what it is. Only I prefer the word "agent" better.

HANNAY. "Secret agent" I suppose? For which country?

ANNABELLA. I have no country.

HANNAY. Born in a balloon, eh?

ANNABELLA. None of your English humour please Mr Hannay! I am being pursued by a very brilliant secret agent of a certain foreign power who is on the point of obtaining top secret and highly confidential information *VITAL* to your air defence. I tracked two of his men to that Music Hall. Unfortunately they recognised me. They are in the street this moment. Beneath your English lamp post.

> (**HANNAY** *lifts the blind. The two* **CLOWNS** *run on as sinister* **HEAVIES.** *They wear trilbies and trench-coats and carry a large 1930s lamppost. They plonk it down. Stand beneath it. Look sinister. Exit with the lamp post.*)

Now do you believe me?

> (**HANNAY** *lifts the blind again. The* **CLOWNS** *run on again with the lamp post. Look sinister.*)

HANNAY. Alright. You win!

> (*The* **CLOWNS** *and lamp-post hastily exit.*)

ANNABELLA. Mr Hannay, I'm going to tell you something now which is not very healthy. It will mean either life. Or death. But if I tell you then you are – inwolved.

HANNAY. In what?

ANNABELLA. Inwolved. Do you vish to be – inwolved?

> (**HANNAY** *turns back to the blind. The* **CLOWNS** *were not expecting this. They rush on again. Plonk down the lamp post. They are getting exhausted.* **HANNAY** *turns.*)

HANNAY. Alright!! Tell me!!!

(The **CLOWNS** *sigh. Heft up the lamp post.*
Rush off again.)

ANNABELLA. Very well. Have you heard of the Thirty-Nine
Steps?

HANNAY. What's that a pub?

ANNABELLA. No more jokes Mr Hannay please! All I can
tell you is these men will stick at NOTHING! If they
are not stopped, it is only of matter of days, perhaps
hours, before the top secret and highly confidential
information is out of the country. And when they've got
it out of the country – God help us all! God help the
world!!

HANNAY. The world!!?

ANNABELLA. The world! And we are the only people who
can stop them! You don't know what they're like Mr
Hannay! How clever their chief is! He has a dozen
names! He can look like a thousand people! But one
thing he cannot disguise. This part of his little finger –

(Lifts **HANNAY**'s *little finger.)*

– is missing. So if ever you should meet a man with no
top joint here – be very careful my friend.

HANNAY. I'll remember that.

ANNABELLA. And Richard? May I call you Richard?

HANNAY. Of course.

ANNABELLA. Richard?

HANNAY. Yes?

ANNABELLA. May I stay the night please? I am most
dreadfully tired.

HANNAY. Of course. You can sleep in my bed. I'll get a
shakedown on the armchair.

ANNABELLA. If you vish.

(She turns.)

And one more thing. I need a map of Scotland.

HANNAY. A map of Scotland? There's a map of Scotland in my room. Under the section – "Scotland."

ANNABELLA. Thank you. There is a man we must visit in Scotland if anything is to be done. By the name of Professor Jordan. An Englishman. At a place called – Alt-na-Shell-achhhhhh.

HANNAY. Alt-na-Shell-achhhhhh!? And the Thirty-Nine –

ANNABELLA. Good night... Richard.

HANNAY. Goodnight... Annabella.

(He gazes after her. She wafts mysteriously into the darkness.)

Hannay's Flat. An Hour Later.

(Haunting music.)

*(**HANNAY** crammed in the armchair, tossing and turning, trying to sleep. **ANNABELLA** looms out of the shadows, holding a map. She whispers huskily.)*

ANNABELLA. Richard? Richard?

HANNAY. Annabella!! Can't you sleep? I can't either.

(She leans over him. Looks like she's about to kiss him.)

Annabella! What are you –

*(She cries out! Collapses across him. A knife in her back. **HANNAY** gasps!)*

ANNABELLA. They got me Richard! They will get you next. Only you can stop them now! Only you can save the world! Run Richard run! To Scotland! Find that place I beg of you! Find Alt – na – shellachhhh!!

(She judders violently on his lap. Dies.)

HANNAY. Golly!

(He squeezes out beneath her body. Wrenches the map from her hand. Opens it out. Pores over it.)

Alt-na – Alt-na – Got it!! *Alt-na-Shellachhhhhhh!!*

(Sound effects: Train whistle.)

Edinburgh Train. Compartment. Day.

(Sound effects: Train rattles along, whistles.)

*(**CLOWNS** are two **BUSINESS MEN** in bowler hats. **HANNAY** opposite with hat over his eyes. They all rock with the rattling train.)*

BUSINESS MAN 1. How's the Mrs?

BUSINESS MAN 2. Fine fanks. How's your Mrs?

BUSINESS MAN 1. Fine fanks.

BUSINESS MAN 2. Funny fings Mrs's!

BUSINESS MAN 1. Can't live wiv 'em!

BUSINESS MAN 2. Can't live wivout 'em!

(They roar with laughter.)

(Sound effects: Whistle.)

Off to Edinburgh!

BUSINESS MAN 1. Here we go!

BUSINESS MAN 2. Where are we now?

BUSINESS MAN 1. I'll have a look.

(He opens the window, rapidly reads the passing signs.)

Nottin'ham... Chippen'am... Birmin'am... Buckin'am... Billin'am... Downton Abbey and 'ere we are! Edinburgh town!

(Sound effects: Brakes screech.)

(They all lurch.)

BUSINESS MAN 2. That was quick!

(Sound effects: Announcer: Edinburgh town! Edinburgh town!)

Edinburgh Station. Day.

BUSINESS MAN 2. Think I'll get a paper.

BUSINESS MAN 1. I'll go to the lavatory.

> *(Gets up, squeezes past.)*

Excuse me. Sorry. Sorry.

BUSINESS MAN 2. Sorry. Sorry.

> *(Bumps into* **HANNAY.***)*

HANNAY. Sorry.

> *(***BUSINESS MAN 1** *exits.* **BUSINESS MAN 2** *gets up. Drops window.* **BUSINESS MAN 1** *reappears as* **PAPERBOY.** *Broad Scottish.)*

PAPERBOY. Paper, paper! Read all aboot it! Read all aboot it!

BUSINESS MAN 2. Evening paper please.

PAPERBOY. Evenin' paper sir? Thankoo sir. *(Gives him a newspaper.)* Evenin' paper. Evenin' paper!

> *(***PAPERBOY** *runs off.)*

PAPERBOY. Evenin' paper! Evenin' paper!

> *(***BUSINESS MAN 2** *sits. Opens newspaper.* **HANNAY** *puts pipe in mouth.* **BUSINESS MAN 1** *returns. Squeezes past knees.)*

BUSINESS MAN 1. 'scuse me. 'scuse me. Sorry. Sorry.

BUSINESS MAN 2. Sorry. Sorry.

HANNAY. Sorry.

BUSINESS MAN 2. *(Reading the first page.)* Good Lord!

BUSINESS MAN 1. What is it?

BUSINESS MAN 2. "Woman murdered in fashionable London West End flat!"

(HANNAY freezes.)

BUSINESS MAN 1. Would you believe it? Go on.

BUSINESS MAN 2. Stabbed in the back. Portland Place. Terrible.

BUSINESS MAN 1. Terrible!

(They look at HANNAY.)

HANNAY. Terrible!

BUSINESS MAN 2. *(Reading.)* "The tenant – Richard Hannay – is missing. Approximately thirty-seven. Wavy hair. Light Brown eyes. Pencil moustache. Pipe."

(HANNAY hides his pipe.)

HANNAY. Excuse me?

BUSINESS MAN 2. Yes?

HANNAY. Might I have a quick look at your paper?

BUSINESS MAN 2. Certainly.

(Hands him the paper.)

Think I'll pop out to the buffet car. Finished?

(Snatches paper back.)

Fancy anythin'? Fancy anythin'?

BUSINESS MAN 1. No thank you.

HANNAY. No thank you.

*(**BUSINESS MAN 2** squeezes past knees.)*

BUSINESS MAN 2. Sorry. Sorry.

BUSINESS MAN 1. Sorry. Sorry.

HANNAY. Sorry.

> (**BUSINESS MAN 2** *leaves the compartment.*
> **BUSINESS MAN 1** *opens the window. Gasps!*)

BUSINESS MAN 1. Good Heavens!!! The station's stiff with police!

> (*Sounds of police car bells.* **HANNAY** *freezes.*
> *Pulls hat over his eyes.*)

Excuse me Constable! Caught the West End murderer yet?

> (**BUSINESS MAN 2** *puts on* **POLICE** *helmet,*
> *appears at the window.*)

POLICEMAN. We'll catch him, don't ye worry sir!

BUSINESS MAN 1. That's the spirit!

> (**POLICEMAN** *changes into* **PORTER**'s *hat.*)

PORTER. All aboard for the Highlands! Next stop the Highlands!

> (*Blows whistle. Changes between* **POLICEMAN**
> *and* **PORTER** *hats.*)

POLICEMAN. Anything suspicious let us know sir!

BUSINESS MAN 1. Will do constable!

PORTER. All aboard! All aboard!

> (*Blows whistle.* **BUSINESS MAN 1** *puts on*
> **PAPERBOY** *hat. Runs round.*)

PAPERBOY. Paper, paper! Read all aboot it! Read all –

BUSINESS MAN 2. (*Pulls on bowler.*) No thank you!

> (**BUSINESS MAN 2** *pulls off bowler, changes*
> *between* **PORTER** *&* **POLICEMAN**.)

PORTER. All aboard! All aboard!

POLICEMAN. Keep your eyes peeled won't you sir!

> (**PAPERBOY** *back in compartment. Pulls on*
> **BUSINESS MAN 1** *bowler.*)

BUSINESS MAN 1. Will do constable!

> (*Pulls off bowler, pulls on* **PAPERBOY** *hat.*
> *Runs round again.*)

PAPERBOY. Paper, paper! Read all aboot it! Read all aboot
it!

PORTER. All aboard! All aboard!

POLICEMAN. Keep your eyes peeled! Keep your eyes
peeled!

> (**BUSINESS MAN 1** *pulls off* **PAPERBOY** *hat,*
> *jumps back into compartment, pulls on*
> **BUSINESS MAN 1** *bowler.*)

BUSINESS MAN 1. Will do constable! Will do constable!

PORTER. All aboard! All aboard!

> (*Blows whistle.* **BUSINESS MAN 1** *pulls on*
> **PAPERBOY** *hat. Runs round.*)

PAPERBOY. Read all aboot it! Read all aboot it!

PORTER. All aboard! All aboard!

> (*Blows whistle.*)

PAPERBOY. Read all aboot it!! Read all aboot it!!

POLICEMAN/PORTER. Keep your eyes peeled! Keep your
eyes peeled! All aboard! All aboard! Ready to depart!
Keep your eyes peeled! Keep your eyes peeled!

PAPERBOY. Final Edition! Final Edition! Final Edition!!

HANNAY. *Oh do get on with it!!*

(Sound effects: Train shrieks. Burst of steam.)

(PORTER, POLICEMAN *&* **PAPERBOY** *run out.* **BUSINESS MAN 1** *and* **2** *sit in the compartment.)*

Highland Train. Compartment. Night.

(Sound effects: Train rattles along.)

BUSINESS MAN 1. Awf we go then!

BUSINESS MAN 2. Awf to the Highlands!

BUSINESS MAN 1. *(Looks into corridor.)* Here! Guess what!?

BUSINESS MAN 2. What?

BUSINESS MAN 1. The police are searching the train!

BUSINESS MAN 2. Searching the train!? Blimey!!

(HANNAY freezes! Leaps up.)

HANNAY. Excuse me!!

(Squeezes past knees.)

Sorry! Sorry!

BUSINESS MAN 1. Sorry.

BUSINESS MAN 2. Sorry.

(HANNAY charges out.)

BUSINESS MAN 1. He's in a rush!

(Sound effects: Train shrieks. roars into tunnel.)

Highland Train. Corridor. Night.

(Lights flash. **HANNAY** *lurches down the corridor, looking behind him.)*

VOICES. Excuse me please. Sorry to disturb ye. Have ye seen this man? His name is Richard Hannay.

*(***HANNAY*** *freezes. More* **VOICES** *coming towards him.)*

Excuse me please. Sorry to disturb ye. Have ye seen this man? His name is Richard Hannay.

*(***HANNAY*** *freezes again, turns desperately this way and that. Suddenly he notices something. He is suddenly entranced.)*

*(***PAMELA*** *romantic music*.)*

---

* A license to produce THE 39 STEPS, ABRIDGED does not include a performance license for any third-party or copyrighted music. Licensees should create an original composition or use music in the public domain. For further information, please see Music Use Note on page 3.

Highland Train. Pamela's Compartment. Night.

(**PAMELA**, *young mid-twenties, is engrossed in a book.* **HANNAY** *gazes at her, entranced. He marches in, sweeps her into his arms.*)

HANNAY. Darling! How lovely to see you!

(*He kisses her passionately. She slaps him.*)

I'm most terribly sorry but they're after me for murder. My name's Richard Hannay and I swear I'm innocent. You've got to help me! You see the safety of this country and the whole world depends upon it –

(*The door opens.* **TWO POLICEMAN** *appear.*)

POLICEMAN 1. Sorry to disturb you sir, madam. But have either of ye have seen this man passing in the last few minutes? His name is Richard Hannay and he's extremely dangerous.

(*He takes out a photograph.* **PAMELA** *looks at it. Looks at* **HANNAY**. *Looks at the photo.*)

PAMELA. Yes! This is the man you want Inspector! He pushed in here and forced himself upon me. He told me his name was Richard Hannay!

POLICEMAN 2. Is your name Richard Hannay?

HANNAY. Certainly not!

POLICEMAN 2. But this young lady clearly stated

(**HANNAY** *pushes open the door. He leaps from the train.*)

(*Sound effects: Train shrieks!!! Deafening and whooshing train sounds.*)

POLICEMAN 1. He's leapt from the train sir!

(They all gasp! Look through the window.)

Oh my God sir! We're on the –

PAMELA. Forth Bridge!

POLICEMAN 2. Don't look miss! After him constable!

POLICEMAN 1. Right you are sir.

*(***POLICEMAN 1*** jumps after ***HANNAY.****)*

(Sound effects: Train shrieks!!! Pounding wheels!!!)

Highland Train. Carriage Exterior. Night.

(**HANNAY** *and* **POLICEMAN 1** *inch their way along the rattling train. It shoots into a tunnel. They appear on the roof. Barely balancing, coats flapping.* **POLICEMAN 2** *and* **PAMELA** *watch gripped at the window.*)

PAMELA. Might I make a suggestion?

POLICEMAN 2. Not now miss.

POLICEMAN 1. *(Lunges.)* Missed him sir!!!

POLICEMAN 2. Missed him miss.

PAMELA. Just pull the communication cord!

POLICEMAN 2. No miss! Whatever you do! Never ever pull the –

(**PAMELA** *pulls the cord.*)

(*Sound effects: Brakes screech. Train halts.*)

(**HANNAY** *and* **POLICEMAN 1** *crash forward. Smoke fills the stage.*)

(*Blackout.*)

Forth Bridge. Night.

(Sound effects: Wind and creaking girders.)

(Lights up on the Forth Bridge. **HANNAY** *is crawling along the top.* **PAMELA** *watches from the train.)*

PAMELA. Look! There he is! *On top of the bridge!!!*

(The **TWO POLICEMAN** *climb after him. They try to grab him. He swings round. A thousand feet above the river.)*

Oh no! Now he's – oh my God! – *under the bridge!!*

HANNAY. Oh crikey!

(He lets go. **PAMELA** *screams. He disappears. A tiny splash.)*

(Blackout.)

RADIO ANNOUNCER. *(Voice over.)* "...the suspect Richard Hannay managed to jump from a train on to the Forth Bridge. Police pursued him but he gave them the slip."

Scottish Moors. Night.

(Sound effects: **POLICE** *whistles, dogs.)*

*(***HANNAY*** *running through the Scottish mist.)*

RADIO ANNOUNCER. *(Voice over continues.)* ..."He is approximately thirty-seven and about six foot one. Although he is clearly dangerous and almost certainly armed, he is quite good looking actually, with wavy hair, light brown eyes and a very attractive pencil moustache...

*(***HANNAY*** *smiles handsomely at us.)*

...he is currently on foot but police are closing in with specialist squads in fugitive apprehension by foot, by road and – by air!"

(Sound effects: The buzz of a plane.)

*(***HANNAY*** *looks up.* **CLOWNS** *chase him with model Tiger Moth plane.)*

(Sound effects: Plane gives chase.)

*(***HANNAY*** *runs for his life.* **CLOWNS** *open fire. Make ack-ack-ack noises.)*

(Sound effects: Machine gun fire.)

*(***HANNAY*** *desperately crawls. Ducks and dives. Dodges the bullets.)*

(Sound effects: Bullets strafe the ground around him.)

*(***HANNAY*** *leaps for his life.* **CLOWNS** *and plane bank too fast, go into tail-spin.)*

(Sound effects: Plane into dizzying dive. Desperately tries to pull out.)

(CLOWNS *with plane crash! Explode!)*

(Sound effects: Explosion in fire and smoke.)

Alt-Na-Shellach. Front Door. Night.

(**HANNAY** *appears! Staggers through smoke.
A gothic front door looms.* **HANNAY** *dives for
the bell-pull.*)

(*Sound effects: Avon chimes: ding-dong!*)

(*The door opens. An aristocratic lady in
tweeds –* **LOUISA JORDAN.**)

MRS JORDAN. Yes?

HANNAY. I am so sorry to disturb you but is this Alt-na-
Shellach? Home of Professor Jordan?

MRS JORDAN. It is. I am the Professor's wife. Louisa
Jordan. May I know your name please?

HANNAY. My name is Hammond. A friend of – Annabella
Schmidt.

MRS JORDAN. Annabella Schmidt? Why do come in Mr
Hammond please.

(**HANNAY** *enters.*)

Alt-Na-Shellach. Professor's Study. Night.

MRS JORDAN. Just in here if you would please. The professor will be with you shortly.

HANNAY. Thank you.

MRS JORDAN. If you wouldn't mind waiting?

HANNAY. Not at all.

> (*She exits.* **PROFESSOR JORDAN** *appears in a fast armchair.*)

PROFESSOR. Mr Hammond! So sorry to have kept you.

HANNAY. It's quite alright.

PROFESSOR. So you're from Annabella Schmidt? Do you have any news?

HANNAY. She's been murdered!

PROFESSOR. Murdered!? Yes of course! The Portland Place affair. And now the police are after you!

HANNAY. I didn't do it you know!

PROFESSOR. Of course you didn't do it, Mr – Hannay. I suppose it's safe to call you by your real name now?

HANNAY. Quite safe.

PROFESSOR. Splendid. So what was it do you think Annabella was trying to tell me?

HANNAY. I believe she was trying to tell you about some vital secret top secret air ministry secret and she was killed by a foreign agent who's after the vital top secret air ministry secret too. But chiefly she was looking for something called – the Thirty-Nine Steps!

PROFESSOR. The Thirty-Nine Steps?

HANNAY. If we can find out what the Thirty-Nine Steps are –

PROFESSOR. So tell me Mr Hannay – did she happen to tell you what this foreign agent looked like?

HANNAY. There wasn't time. Ah yes! Wait! There was one thing. Part of his little finger is missing.

PROFESSOR. Which little finger?

HANNAY. This one I think. *(Holds up a little finger.)*

PROFESSOR. Are you sure it wasn't – this one? *(Holds up his own little finger. It is cut off at the knuckle.)*

(Holds up little stump.)

– this little finger?

HANNAY. I'm not sure . I think—

(Sees the stump. He gasps! The **PROFESSOR** *pulls out a revolver.)*

PROFESSOR. Mr Hannay. I'm afraid you've forced me into a very difficult position. You see I live here as a respectable citizen. My very best friend is the Sheriff of the County. So my whole existence could be seriously jeopardised if it became known that I was not – shall we say – what I seem. But what makes it doubly important that I simply cannot let you go is that I am indeed about to convey some very vital top secret information out of the country. Oh yes! I've got it alright. I'm afraid poor Annabella Schmidt would have been far too late. So it seems there is only one option.

(Aims revolver.)

Unless of course – you care to join us.

HANNAY. Join you?

PROFESSOR. You see you're just the kind of man we need. Sharp. Intelligent. Cold-blooded. Ruthless. When the war comes these will be the exact qualities we need.

HANNAY. War?

PROFESSOR. Oh yes indeed. We'll have quite a show of it. But this time – we'll win!

HANNAY. And what if I don't believe in those qualities?

PROFESSOR. What other qualities are there?

HANNAY. Decency, selflessness, goodness... love?

PROFESSOR. *LOVE!!!?* Oh please Mr Hannay! When have you ever *loved* anyone? It's not in your nature, old sport! Never has been, has it? You have no heart you see! That is why you are so alone. In your dull little rented Portland Place flat.

HANNAY. How the HELL do you know about –

PROFESSOR. Oh we know you very well old chap! Such a sad story. So terribly terribly sad. No home of your own. No-one to share it with! So alone! So lost! But you don't need to be you see! There is a home – And many many to share it with! Many many many many Hannay! The home – or heim – of the Masters mein liebling!!

> (**HANNAY** *gasps. The* **PROFESSOR** *is clearly a card-carrying Nazi!*)

Come with us my dear! As we crush the world! In our mighty fist! Crush all the little people, the tiny people! The insignificant people! With all their outmoded sentimental notions! Decency and goodness and – love! Ha ha ha ha!! Join *US* Hannay! The Master Race! To whom all the people of the world will bow! On our great unstoppable march of ruthlessness and power! Commanded eternally by destiny itself! Well old sport? What do you say? Will you join us Richard!?

> (**HANNAY** *thinks.*)

HANNAY. Alright Professor! If you think I'm suitable material.

PROFESSOR. Oh yes! YES YES YES! I do I do old sport! How utterly unutterably utterly wunderbar!

HANNAY. Oh just one thing. One little tiny question. Before I – sign up.

PROFESSOR. Of course! Ask away! Ask away!

HANNAY. What exactly are – the Thirty-Nine Steps?

PROFESSOR. The Thirty-Nine Steps! Ha ha ha! Though I say so meinself – is my own brilliant idea!!! The very soul of the enterprise! Ha Ha Ha!!!!

> *(Stops! Gasps!)*

Wait! Wait a MINUTE! You thought you could join us and zen ask ze questions! Ha!!! You – zink you can pull ze vool?

HANNAY. Master Race? I despise you!

PROFESSOR. Accchh! You are as bad as she was! Annabella Schmidt!!! With all her high-minded *LOVE OF ZE PEOPLE! ALL HER DEMOKRATIKISCH BOVENSHEISSEDRIVVLE!* I thought for a moment you might – But no! NO!!! You want to know what are the Thirty-Nine Steps? But let me tell you Hannay, The Thirty-Nine Steps? You will never ever EVER KNOW!

> *(He aims the revolver. Opens the door. Calls.)*

Mrs Jordan?

MRS JORDAN. *(Offstage.)* Yes dear?

PROFESSOR. Mr Hannay is just saying goodbye dear.

MRS JORDAN. *(Offstage.)* Goodbye Mr Hannay.

HANNAY. Goodbye. Or rather *AUF WIEDERSEHEN!!!!!!*

> *(HANNAY dives at the PROFESSOR.)*

(Sound effects: Gun shots. Smashed glass.)

(Blackout.)

(Sound effects: Fight. Smashed furniture. **MRS JORDAN***'s voice.)*

MRS JORDAN. *Get him Heinrich!! GET HIM!! GET THE SCHWEIN!! SCHWEIN! SCHWEIN! SCHWEIN!!*

(Fight music. Builds and cuts.)

Sheriff's Office. Night.

(The SHERIFF at his desk. Laughing loudly. A telephone on the desk. A window. MAN looks out of it.)

SHERIFF. And to think the villain called me his friend! Whereas all along he was –

(The MAN turns. It is HANNAY. A little worse for wear but still in one piece.)

HANNAY. A spy!

SHERIFF. A spy! Ay!!! Tea, Mr Hannay?

HANNAY. No tea for me, thank you

SHERIFF. Biscuit?

HANNAY. No biscuit thank you! Look here, sheriff, I don't want to rush you or anything but shouldn't we be taking steps? This is serious you know! Otherwise you don't think I'd have put myself in your hands with a murder charge hanging over me?

SHERIFF. Ach! Never heed the murder Mr Hannay! You've convinced me of your innocence right enough. We just need a quick statement to forward to the proper authorities.

(Picks up phone.)

Whenever you're ready Inspector!

HANNAY. Statement! There's no time for a statement! The professor's got the information, don't you see? And it's absolutely vital to the safety of our air –

SHERIFF. Hurry Inspector please!

(INSPECTOR bursts in.)

About time man! Do you think I enjoy playing for time with a *MURDERER!!!*

HANNAY. *MURDERER???*

SHERIFF. *MURDERER!!!* Richard Hannay, you are under arrest! For the wilful murder of Annabella Schmidt in Flat Seven, Portland Place, London on Tuesday last. Take him to the County Gaol!

INSPECTOR. Rightaway sir!

HANNAY. But you heard my story! It's true! Every word of it!

SHERIFF. Listen Hannay! We're not such imbeciles in Scotland as some smart Londoners may think! I don't believe your cock-and-bull story about the professor! Why, Professor Jordan is my best friend in the district!

    (Picks up phone.)

Get me Professor Jordan!

    (To **HANNAY.***)*

You're in deadly deep water Mr Hannay! And it's getting deadlier and deepier by the second!

VOICE. *(Phone.)* Hello hello hello hello?

    *(***SHERIFF** *and* **INSPECTOR** *look at each other. Look for the voice, run round the office. Realise the voice is coming from the phone.)*

SHERIFF. Yes!!!? Who is that!? This is the Sheriff of the County here and I'll thank you to – sorry? Ach!

    (Bows.)

Professor! I do beg your pardon most truly humbly sir. So so so so terribly sorry sir. Just to let you know sir we have apprehended the villain sir. Richard Hannay sir! Handcuffs Inspector please!

INSPECTOR. Right away sir yessir!

> (*Grabs* **HANNAY**, *clicks handcuff on his wrist.*)

Come along quietly sir, please sir.

SHERIFF. (*On phone.*) Handcuffs going on now sir.

HANNAY. *I don't think so Inspector!*

> (*Knocks the* **INSPECTOR** *to the floor. Leaps spectacularly out of the window.*)

> (*Sound effects: Breaking glass. Cars swerve to stop.*)

INSPECTOR. He's leapt from the window sir! He's escaping!! Stop him!! Stop that man!!

> (**HANNAY** *runs out straddling the window. The* **INSPECTOR** *charges after him, blowing his whistle.*)

VOICE. (*Phone.*) Hello hello hello HELLO!!?

SHERIFF. (*Picks up phone.*) Ah professor! Helloo there! Just to say sir everything's all tickety boo sir! Oh yes indeed sir! Indeedy indeedy indeedy it is sir!

> (*Laughs in terror. Blows whistle. Runs out. Still holding the phone.*)

> (*Chase music.*)

> (*Lights fast fade.*)

---

* A license to produce THE 39 STEPS, ABRIDGED does not include a performance license for any third-party or copyrighted music. Licensees should create an original composition or use music in the public domain. For further information, please see Music Use Note on page 3.

Scottish Streets. Night.

(Sound effects: **POLICE** *whistles/shouting.)*

*(***HANNAY*** *running through the dark city streets.)*

(Searchlights, torches and shadows chase him. He stops. Listens.)

MUSIC: ["SCOTLAND THE BRAVE"]

(The clowns march on as a Scottish marching band. **HANNAY** *nips in, marches with them, looks anxiously back at his pursuers.)*

Assembly Hall. Scotland. Night.

(A banner across the back of the stage: VOTE McCORQUODALE. A very old man **MR DUNWOODY** *enters with a chair and lectern.* **HANNAY** *bursts in breathless.)*

HANNAY. Excuse me! Sorry! I wonder if you could possibly –

DUNWOODY. Why!!! It's you!! Helloo! Helloo! Ye're here at last!

HANNAY. Am I?

DUNWOODY. He's here Mr McQuarrie! Mr McQuarrie!!!

(Enter **MR MCQUARRIE.** *Another even older man.)*

MCQUARRIE. Ach! He's here! Thank the Lord! Thank the Lord!

*(***MCQUARRIE:***)*

(The old men grab **HANNAY,** *plonk him in the chair, straighten his tie.* **DUNWOODY** *carries the lectern to the front of the stage.)*

(Sound effects: Applause.)

DUNWOODY. Thankee thankee! I shall now call upon our ever popular chairman Mr McQuarrie to introduce this evening's special guest speaker! Mr McQuarrie if you would please?

*(***MCQUARRIE** *hobbles toward the lectern. He speaks entirely inaudibly.)*

MR MCQUARRIE. Thankee... thankee... ladies and gentlemen... allow me now to introduce our special –

DUNWOODY. Speak up Mr McQuarrie sir.

MCQUARRIE. Speak up?

DUNWOODY. Speak up. Ay.

MCQUARRIE. *(Even less audibly.)* – special guest speaker. Whose brilliant record as soldier, statesman, pioneer and poet speak louder than words. Which is more than can be said for me.

> *(He laughs uproariously.)*

So – without further ado – ladies and gentlemen, welcome please tonight's illustrious special guest speaker – Captain Rob Roy McAlistair!

> *(Sound effects: Applause.)*

> *(The old men nod at **HANNAY**. **HANNAY** sits there smiling. He looks round for Captain McAlistair. Realises they mean him. Looks aghast. He marches to the lectern.)*

HANNAY. Well – ladies and gentlemen I must apologise for my slight hesitation in addressing you just now but to tell you the simple truth, I'd entirely failed while listening to the chairman's flattering description, to realise he was talking about me.

> *(Sound effects: Laughter.)*

Thanks so much! Anyway – little did I realise – when I came up to Scotland over that magnificent structure the Forth Bridge – how delighted I would feel to be addressing such an historic gathering. And in particular how relieved I am to find myself so happily delivered of the cares and anxieties that are so often the lot of a man in my position.

> *(Accidentally reveals handcuff. Hurriedly hides it.)*

So tonight we're here – as you know – to discuss –

(**PAMELA** *enters.*)

HANNAY. Oh hello. Do take a seat – good heavens! Hello!

PAMELA. Hello!

(*Romantic* **PAMELA** *music.**)

(*They gaze at each other. She runs out.* **HANNAY** *gazes after her.*)

(*Romantic music: Cuts.*)

HANNAY. – to discuss – um – what shall we discuss? I know. How about the idle rich! Not that I can talk about that because I'm not rich and I've never been idle.

(*Sound effects: Laughter.*)

In fact most of my life I've been pretty busy really. Well not recently. Recently I've been in a bit of a slump. Well not that recently. Recently, the last few days, well the last *day* actually, everything's gone a bit um –

(**PAMELA** *re-enters. Whispers furiously to* **MACQUARRIE** *and* **DUNWOODY**. *They gasp! Exit hurriedly.* **HANNAY** *keeps going.*)

– haywire frankly. Pretty damn difficult actually.

But you know the odd thing is – *the odd thing is* – you carry on! And it's pretty bloody bracing when you do. There's no time to think. And your mind's singing! And your heart's racing! Racing like the – Flying Scotsman! And you suddenly realise – you care! About the world!

---

* A license to produce THE 39 STEPS, ABRIDGED does not include a performance license for any third-party or copyrighted music. Licensees should create an original composition or use music in the public domain. For further information, please see Music Use Note on page 3.

And the people in the world. And people are pretty damn good things when you think about it. They're not little. Or tiny. Or insignificant. Because they know what's right.

> (**PAMELA** *re-enters. With the two* **HEAVIES** *in trilbies and trench-coats. They come up behind* **HANNAY**. **HANNAY** *sees them but keeps going.*)

And they fight for it. That's right! They do! If they need to. Not for ruthlessness and power.

> **MUSIC**: Charles Hubert Hastings Parry's **["JERUSALEM"]**

But for goodness and decency and – yes alright. Love! Is that such an – "outmoded sxental notion"? Well is it? So look here! Let's make a new world! A happier world! Where no neighbour plots against neighbour! Where no nation plots against nation! Where there's no persecution or –

> (*The* **HEAVIES** *and* **PAMELA** *get closer and closer.*)

– hunting down! A world where suspicion and cruelty and fear have been forever banished! That's something worth fighting for! Well isn't it!? So I'm asking you – each and every one of you. You! And you! And you!

> (*He points to different members of the audience. He speeds up.*)

> **MUSIC**: Charles Hubert Hastings Parry's **["JERUSALEM"]** – *Speeds up*

And you! And you too! And definitely *you!* Is that the sort of world you want? Because that's the sort of world I want! What do you think? Let's vote on it! Come on everyone! Vote for a brave world! A new world! For a better world! And above all for –

(Looks up at the banner.)

– Mr McCrocodile!! Thank you.

> **MUSIC:** Charles Hubert Hastings Parry's **["JERUSALEM"]** – *Climaxes*

> *(Sound effects: Tumultuous applause.)*

> *(**PAMELA** points at **HANNAY**.)*

PAMELA. This is the man you want Inspector!

HANNAY. Where have I heard those words before?

> *(**HANNAY** makes a bolt for it. The **HEAVIES** grab him. Snap the handcuff on his other wrist.)*

I suppose you think you've been damn clever! Don't you see I was speaking the truth in that railway carriage! You must have seen I was genuine!

PAMELA. Goodbye Mr Hannay. And good riddance!

HANNAY. Alright then just listen! There's an enormously important secret –

HEAVY 1. That'll do now!

HANNAY. – being taken out of this country by a devilishly brilliant foreign agent! I can't do anything myself because of these fool detectives! But if you telephone Scotland Yard immediately –

PAMELA. I'll do no such thing!

HEAVY 2. Actually miss, beg pardon miss, we should like you to come too miss.

PAMELA. Me? But –

HEAVY 1. He's to be questioned by the Procurator Fiscal personally.

PAMELA. Procurator Fiscal personally?

HEAVY 2. We need you as a witness miss.

PAMELA. Need me as a witness?

HEAVY 1. Just climb into the car miss?

PAMELA. Car?

> *(They've forgotten to make the car. They grab chairs. Build the car. **HEAVY 1** sits. Turns the key.)*

> *(Sound effects: Motorcar noises.)*

HEAVY 2. After you miss.

> *(**PAMELA** climbs into the back seat. **HANNAY** pushed in beside her. **HEAVY 2** climbs in beside **HEAVY 1**. **HANNAY** delighted to see **PAMELA**.)*

HANNAY. Hello!

PAMELA. I'm not talking to you.

HANNAY. Right.

> *(**HANNAY** whistles chirpily. **PAMELA** sighs.)*

Police Car. Highlands. Night.

(Driving music.)*

(Sound effects: Car revs, tyres screech.)

(They lurch along winding roads.)

HANNAY. Will you have a small bet with me Pamela?

(PAMELA scowls.)

Alright I'll have it with you Sherlock. I'll lay you a hundred to one that your Procurator Fiscal has the top joint of his little finger missing.

(HEAVY 1 whacks HANNAY. PAMELA gasps. HANNAY grins.)

I win.

(Sound effects: Car brakes screech.)

(Car lurches to a stop.)

---

* A license to produce THE 39 STEPS, ABRIDGED does not include a performance license for any third-party or copyrighted music. Licensees should create an original composition or use music in the public domain. For further information, please see Music Use Note on page 3.

Moorland Road. Night.

PAMELA. What are we stopping for?

> *(Sound effects: Bleating sheep sounds.)*

HEAVY 2. Damned sheep! We'll have to clear 'em away!

HANNAY. Well well! A whole flock of detectives.

HEAVY 1. What do we do with him?

HEAVY 2. Here's what we do with him!

> *(Grabs* **HANNAY**'s *handcuff. Unlocks it, snaps it on to* **PAMELA**.)

PAMELA. What on earth are you doing! Unchain this handcuff!

HEAVY 2. Now you're a special constable miss. As long as you stay – he stays! Come on man!

> *(They jump out. Exit chasing sheep.)*

Out of the way ye bleating brutes!

HANNAY. And as long as I go – you go. *COME ON!*

> *(**HANNAY** jumps out of the car. Pulls her after him.)*

PAMELA. What are you doing!??? Help! Help!! HELP!!

HANNAY. Now you listen to me!

> *(He takes his pipe. Sticks it in her back.)*

Feel this – *pistol?*

PAMELA. Yes!

HANNAY. Do you want me to shoot you stone dead?

PAMELA. Not particularly no.

HANNAY. Then get a move on!

(HANNAY *drags her after him.*)

PAMELA. Ow!!

(*They exit.*)

(*The* HEAVIES *return.*)

HEAVY 2. They got away! Dammit!!

(*Jumps in car. Turns key.*)

Battery's flat! What do we do?

HEAVY 1. Find the professor!

HEAVY 2. What about the car?

HEAVY 1. Carry the car. Come on!

(HEAVY 1 *exits.* HEAVY 2 *picks up all the chairs. Staggers off after him. The chairs clatter off stage.*)

Dark Moors. Night.

(HANNAY and PAMELA appear.)

PAMELA. Now where are we?

HANNAY. No idea! Come on!

PAMELA. Not across that horrid smelly bog!

HANNAY. Afraid so! Sorry!

(HANNAY pulls her. She sinks.)

(Sound effects: Squelch!)

PAMELA. I can't move!

HANNAY. Yes you can! COME ON!

(He pulls her.)

(Sound effects: Squelch!)

PAMELA. Ow!

(Sound effects: POLICE whistles. Dogs barking.)

HANNAY. Quick! Under this – waterfall!!

(Calls off-stage.)

Come on!

(CLOWN 1 runs on with a shower curtain which he jiggles.)

(Sound effects: Waterfall.)

(HANNAY pulls PAMELA behind the shower curtain. CLOWN 2 in police helmet runs past blowing his whistle. PAMELA jumps out.)

PAMELA. Help! HEEELP!

HANNAY. Now listen to me! One more peep out of you –

(Pushes pipe into her ribs.)

– I'll shoot you first and myself after. I mean it! Right! Come on! Over these boulders!

(Calls off-stage.)

Boulders!

> *(CLOWNS run on. They make themselves into boulders. HANNAY hauls PAMELA over them. The CLOWNS groan. HANNAY jumps off. Pulls PAMELA after him. The clowns gasp with relief and run off. HANNAY and PAMELA trudge on. He whistles happily.)*

PAMELA. I don't know what you're so happy about! You'll never escape you know! What chance have you got tied to me?

HANNAY. I'd keep that question for your husband if I were you.

PAMELA. I don't have a husband!

HANNAY. Lucky him! Come along!

PAMELA. Listen, Richard Hannay, those policemen will catch you as soon as it's light. You know that, don't you?

HANNAY. Listen, Pamela whatever your name is –

PAMELA. Edwards.

HANNAY. Edwards. You don't know Schnozzle Edwards?

PAMELA. NO!!!

HANNAY. Funny you look just like him. I keep telling you those policemen are not policemen!

PAMELA. So you're still sticking to your silly penny novelette spy story!?

HANNAY. Twenty million women on this island! And I've got to be chained to you! I will say this one more time and I am telling you the truth! There's a dangerous conspiracy against this country and we're the only people who can stop it!

PAMELA. The gallant knight to the rescue!

HANNAY. Alright then! You're alone on a dark moor, manacled to a murderer who'll stop at nothing to get you off his hands! If that's the situation you'd prefer then have it my girl and welcome!

(They stop sharp.)

(Sound effects: Running River.)

PAMELA. I am not crossing that – that – that –

(Glares off stage and beckons.)

– river!

(The clowns run on with a cloth that they proceed to ripple.)

HANNAY. It's only a stream!

PAMELA. It's a roaring torrent! Take me back!

HANNAY. There's no turning back now. Sorry. Come on!

(He picks her up. Wades into the river.)

PAMELA. Put me down!!

(The CLOWNS lift the cloth too high.)

HANNAY. Put it down!

PAMELA. Put me down!

HANNAY. Put it DOWN!

PAMELA. I said put me down!

HANNAY. I'm trying to!

> *(Shouts at the* **CLOWNS.***)*

Get off!

> *(The clowns drop the cloth. Run off.* **HANNAY**
> *plonks* **PAMELA** *down.)*

There. Better now?

PAMELA. Thank you!

> *(Sound effects: Crack of thunder. Lightning.*
> *Sudden downpour.)*

Oh no!!!

HANNAY. *(Pulls her.)* Come ON!!!

PAMELA. NO! That's it! I've had it with you! I'm not
moving another inch and that's final!!

HANNAY. *WE'RE IN THE MIDDLE OF A
THUNDERSTORM!!*

PAMELA. *SO!!!?*

HANNAY. *COME ON!!!*

> *(He yanks the handcuff.)*

PAMELA. *OW!!!* You don't care do you!? Look at me! Cold,
miserable, my wrist hurts, it's pouring with rain, I
didn't do anything to hurt you! And all you care about
is your horrible, selfish, pompous, horrible, beastly,
heartless heartless heartless self!

HANNAY. Yes well that's the kind of man I am I'm afraid.

PAMELA. Well God help your wife that's all I can say!

HANNAY. Yes God help her!

PAMELA. Help! Help! HEEEELP!

HANNAY. *LISTEN! IF YOU DON'T SHUT UP – I'LL*
– I'LL –

> *(Sound effects: Bagpipe music.)*

> *(The clowns enter as* **MR** *and* **MRS**
> **MCGARRIGLE.** **MRS MCGARRIGLE** *pushes on a*
> *door with 'HOTEL' above it.* **MR MCGARRIGLE**
> *plays bagpipes.)*

Look! A little tiny little Highland Hotel! Saved by a
bagpipe!

MRS MCGARRIGLE. Ach ye poor wee dears! Come in, come
in, come in! Ooota the terrible storm!

> *(Sound effects: Storm stops.)*

McGarrigle Hotel. Highlands. Night.

HANNAY. Thank you so much.

PAMELA. Thank you.

MRS MCGARRIGLE. Here we are, here we are, here we are, and welcome to the McGarrigle Hotel! I am Mrs McGarrigle. And this is my husband Willie McGarrigle. Willie?

MR MCGARRIGLE. Ay?

MRS MCGARRIGLE. That's enough

(*MR MCGARRIGLE stops playing.*)

So straight awa' wi' ye to your soft warm bed and a fine roaring fire!

HANNAY. Marvellous! Come along darling.

PAMELA. Actually –

(*Everyone freezes.*)

MRS MCGARRIGLE. What is it dearie? Is anything wrong?

HANNAY. Course there's nothing wrong is there darling? She wants to tell you something that's all, don't you my darling? She wants to tell you we're – a runaway couple.

MRS MCGARRIGLE. A runaway – I thought ye were! I thought ye were! Och the romance! The romance of it!

(*MR MCGARRIGLE plays* ["WEDDING MARCH"].)

That's enough Willie.

(*MR MCGARRIGLE stops playing.*)

MRS MCGARRIGLE. Well your secret's safe wi' us. And you're in luck tonight. Cos we've just the one little tiny room left. With just the one little tiny little bed in it.

(She opens the door. A very small bed and a fireplace.)

Now you can snuggle up. Warm as little haggises! Willie!

MR MCGARRIGLE. Ay?

MRS MCGARRIGLE. Fine roaring fire!

(Willie kicks the fireplace. It bursts into flame.)

HANNAY. Lovely! Isn't it darling?

PAMELA. Lovely.

(Sneezes.)

MRS MCGARRIGLE. Make sure she takes that wet skirt off.

HANNAY. I certainly will. Goodnight.

MRS MCGARRIGLE. Willie?

MR MCGARRIGLE. Aye?

MRS MCGARRIGLE. *OOT!*

MR MCGARRIGLE. *OOT!*

(She pulls him out. Slams the door.)

McGarrigle Hotel. Bedroom. Night.

PAMELA. I'm not taking anything off thank you! And if you think I'm going to spend –

> *(Sneezes.)*

Actually I will take my shoes off.

> *(Takes her shoes off.)*

And my stockings.

> *(She undoes her stockings. Tries to remove them. Their handcuffed hands get in the way.)*

HANNAY. Can I be of assistance?

PAMELA. No thank you.

> *(He looks away discretely. She gets the stockings off. Hangs them by the fire. Rubs her hands. He rubs them too. They are both embarrassed.)*

HANNAY. Warmer now?

PAMELA. Yes thanks.

HANNAY. Jolly good.

> *(He leads her to the bed. She follows contentedly. Suddenly realises what she's doing.)*

PAMELA. *WAIT! What are you doing!!?*

HANNAY. Going to bed.

PAMELA. I am not lying on that bed!

HANNAY. I'm afraid you have to rather. Sorry.

(**HANNAY** *climbs on the bed. She has to climb
on too. They lie side by side. He whistles.*)

PAMELA. *Will you please stop whistling!*

HANNAY. I wish I could get that damn tune out of my
head. D'you know when I last slept in a bed? Saturday
night. Whenever that was.

PAMELA. What woke you? Dreams? I imagine murderers
have terrible dreams.

HANNAY. Oh I used to. When I first took to a life of crime,
I used to wake in the middle of the night thinking the
police were after me. Funny that! Just think – in years
to come, you'll be able to take your grandchildren to
Madame Tussauds and point me out.

PAMELA. Which section?

HANNAY. Inveterate no-hopers. Wedded to a life of crime.
That's me Pamela my darling. And the sad story of my
life. Poor little orphan boy who never had a chance.
Irredeemable. Irreclaimable. Unreformable.

PAMELA. Utterly heartless.

HANNAY. Exactly. I'd get away from me as quick as you
can if I were you! Oh no, you can't, can you? Oh well.

> (**HANNAY** *snores loudly. She gazes at him
> tenderly for a moment. Gets a grip. Grabs
> the handcuff. Twists it painfully. Wrenches
> it off. Jumps out of bed. Puts her hand in his
> pocket. Pulls out the pipe. Realises it's not a
> pistol. Slams it furiously on the mantelpiece.
> Exits.*)

McGarrigle Hotel. Telephone Box. Night.

(The **CLOWNS** *are the two* **HEAVIES** *again. Crushed painfully into the hotel telephone box. One talks urgently into the phone. The other listens in. He does* **MRS JORDAN***'s voice behind his hat.)*

HEAVY 1. Mrs Jordan! Listen please! Mrs Jordan!

HEAVY 2. *(Inaudible shrieks!)*

*(***PAMELA** *enters. She listens.)*

HEAVY 1. We *had* to take the girl as well as Hannay! Now he'll have told her the whole plot! She'll know we're not the real police!

*(***PAMELA** *gasps!)*

HEAVY 2. *(Inaudible shrieks!)*

HEAVY 1. What was that Mrs Jordan? Sorry? Dispose of 'em as soon as we find 'em!? Right you are Mrs Jordan!

HEAVY 2. *(Inaudible shrieks!)*

HEAVY 1. What was that madam? He's what? Has he? Is he? Does he? Very good madam! Thank you madam! Goodbye madam!

(Slams down receiver.)

HEAVY 2. What did she say? Spill the beans!

HEAVY 1. The professor's clearin' out! Reckons it's too dangerous with Hannay and the girl on the loose. He's warnin' the whole Thirty-Nine Steps!

HEAVY 2. The whole Thirty-Nine Steps!!? Blimey!! Will he have the – you know? Information?

HEAVY 1. Certainly will! He's picking up our friend from the London Palladium. TONIGHT!

HEAVY 2. TONIGHT!? COME ON THEN!!!

>   *(The* **HEAVIES** *jam on their trilbies. Exit.)*
>
>   *(Sound effects: Car starts. Roars away.)*

McGarrigle Hotel. Bedroom. Dawn.

(HANNAY *is wide awake.* PAMELA *anguished.*)

HANNAY. I *know* they're not policemen! I *said* they weren't policemen!

PAMELA. Sorry.

HANNAY. So what did they say?

PAMELA. Oh – um – yes! Something with a number. Twenty... thirty... that's it! Thirty!

HANNAY. Nine!

PAMELA. Thirty-*Nine!* That's right. Thirty – nine –

HANNAY. Steps!!!

PAMELA. *Thirty-Nine Steps!* How did you know that? Anyway someone's going to warn them! How can you warn steps?

HANNAY. WHAT!? Never mind. Go on!

PAMELA. Right – and – oh yes! Someone's got the wind up and is clearing out. With the information –

HANNAY. With the information? What information?

PAMELA. I don't know. But they're picking someone up from the London Palladium.

HANNAY. Who?

PAMELA. Someone!

HANNAY. London Palladium? With the information? Who's clearing out? Is that the Professor?

PAMELA. Professor!? What professor!?

HANNAY. Our friend with the little finger missing? What's he want to go there for? Funny thing for a master-spy to do!

PAMELA. I do feel such an awful fool for not having believed you.

HANNAY. That's alright.

> *(He smiles. They are sitting very close. They gaze at each other.)*

> *(Romantic music.*)*

So – um –

PAMELA. Yes?

HANNAY. Which room are they staying in?

PAMELA. Who?

HANNAY. Those two men.

PAMELA. Well they're not.

> *(They inch closer and closer.)*

HANNAY. Sorry?

PAMELA. They went away as soon as they'd telephoned. Drove off into the night. Rather fast actually.

HANNAY. Where?

PAMELA. Don't know. Sorry. Does it matter?

> *(They are about to kiss. **HANNAY** leaps up.)*

HANNAY. *DOES IT MATTER!!!???*

> *(Music cuts out.)*

PAMELA. *WHAT!!?*

HANNAY. *Why didn't you stop them!!!???*

---

* A license to produce THE 39 STEPS, ABRIDGED does not include a performance license for any third-party or copyrighted music. Licensees should create an original composition or use music in the public domain. For further information, please see Music Use Note on page 3.

PAMELA. *Because I wanted to see you!!*

HANNAY. *Well that was a stupid thing to do wasn't it??!!!*

PAMELA. *Apparently yes!!!*

HANNAY. So where did they go!!?

PAMELA. I don't know! The London Palladium I suppose!

HANNAY. The London Palladium!? When!!?

PAMELA. Tonight!

HANNAY. TONIGHT!!??

PAMELA. But if they're leaving the country that's fine isn't it?

HANNAY. *FINE!? FINE!!?* I am accused of murder! The only way to clear my name is to expose these spies!

PAMELA. *Your* name! *YOUR* name! You see! All you think about is your *SELF!* Your horrible beastly horrid selfish pompous horrible heartless heartless heartless –

HANNAY. But *MUCH* more important than *THAT* is that they are about to leave the country with – that's it! – top secret and highly confidential information from the Air Ministry! Not only vital to the safety and future of this country's air defence, but of *THE WHOLE WORLD!*

PAMELA. WELL I'M VERY VERY VERY SORRY!!!

HANNAY. SO THANKS FOR YOUR HELP! GOODBYE!!!

PAMELA. GOODBYE!!! AND DON'T EXPECT ME TO COME WITH YOU!!!

HANNAY. I WON'T!!!

PAMELA. I'M NOT SURPRISED YOU'RE AN ORPHAN!

(**HANNAY** *storms out. Slams the door.* **PAMELA** *bursts into tears.*)

Road to London. Night.

(Sound effects: Screeching tyres.)

(Lights up on **HANNAY**. *Motoring goggles. Furiously driving.)*

Telephone Box. London. Night.

PAMELA. Hello. Scotland Yard? I need to speak to the Chief Commissioner please! It's Pamela Edwards here and it's terribly urgent! Oh hello Uncle Bob is that you? Fine thanks! Now look, about Richard Hannay! What? Yes I do actually. Long story. Anyway – he's gone to the – is it okay to tell you? Sorry Uncle Bob. To the – London Palladium!

> MUSIC: ["LONDON PALLADIUM THEME SONG"]*

* A license to produce THE 39 STEPS, ABRIDGED does not include a performance license for any third-party or copyrighted music. Licensees should create an original composition or use music in the public domain. For further information, please see Music Use Note on page 3.

London Palladium. Stage. Night.

RECORDED VOICE. This is the London Palladium!

> (**HANNAY** *appears in a theatre box. Staring through binoculars.* **PAMELA** *appears behind him.*)

PAMELA. Hello.

> (**HANNAY** *spins round. Delighted to see her but acts cross.*)

HANNAY. What on earth are you doing here?

PAMELA. I'll go then shall I?

HANNAY. Er no – better stay now you're here.

PAMELA. Righto.

HANNAY. But now look here! I've found him!

PAMELA. Who?

HANNAY. The Professor. There! In the box.

PAMELA. Gosh yes! But you can't do anything about it!

HANNAY. What!?

PAMELA. I've spoken to Scotland Yard.

HANNAY. Scotland Yard!!!?

PAMELA. My uncle's Chief Commissioner. Uncle Bob.

HANNAY. Bob?

PAMELA. That's right.

HANNAY. Bob's your uncle?

PAMELA. Yes. And he said no top secret highly confidential information's been stolen from the Air Ministry.

HANNAY. But you heard those men say the Professor's got it!

PAMELA. Well they've checked and they're absolutely certain!

HANNAY. *(Looks at audience. Gasps!)* Oh my God! POLICE! You didn't tell them I was here did you?

PAMELA. Oh dear!

HANNAY. Well that's it then. That's IT!!!!!

PAMELA. Sorry.

MUSIC: ["MR MEMORY THEME"]

HANNAY. Wait a minute! That's the damn tune I couldn't get out of my head!

*(**COMPERE** and **MR MEMORY** enter.)*

COMPERE. Good evenin' ladies and gentlemen. And now introducin' one of the most remarkable men ever in the whole world. Mr Memory!

*(**MR MEMORY** bows.)*

(Sound effects: Applause.)

HANNAY. Mr Memory!!

COMPERE. Are you quite ready for the questions Mr Memory?

MEMORY. Quite ready thankoo. I will now place my inner bein' in a state of mental readiness for this evenin's performance. Thankoo.

MUSIC: ["DRUMROLL"]

*(**COMPERE** exits. **MEMORY** goes into a trance-like state. He looks up at the **PROFESSOR**'s box. **HANNAY** swings his binoculars to the*

box. The **PROFESSOR** *signals to* **MEMORY.**
MEMORY *nods to the* **PROFESSOR.***)*

HANNAY. I've got it! Of course they don't think anything's
missing! All the Top Secret information's in Memory's
head! That's why the Professor's here tonight. To take
Memory out of the country!

MEMORY. First question please!! Beg pardon sir? How
high is St Paul's Cathedral? St Paul's Cathedral is –

(**SUPERINTENDANT ALBRIGHT** *enters.*)

(Sound effects: Audience gasp!)

ALBRIGHT. Sorry to disturb the show ladies and gents.
Richard Charles Arbuthnot Hannay?

HANNAY. Yes?

ALBRIGHT. I am Detective Chief Superintendent Albright
sir. New Scotland Yard sir. I am arresting you on a
charge of MURDER!

(Sound effects: Audience gasp!)

HANNAY & PAMELA. *MURDER!?*

PAMELA. But you don't understand Chief Superintendent
Chief Inspector Detective Albright!

ALBRIGHT. Come along quietly there's a good chap sir.

HANNAY. Alright alright Albright.

PAMELA. He's innocent I tell you!

ALBRIGHT. If you don't mind miss.

HANNAY. I'm sorry Pamela there's – no other way!

(Winks at her. Nips behind curtain.)

ALBRIGHT. Very wise sir. Now if you'd just – Wait! Hang on! He's escaped!! QUICK!! Block all the exits!! Carry on as normal Mr Memory if you would please sir.

(**ALBRIGHT** *rushes out.*)

MEMORY. Very good sir. So where was we? Ah yes. St Paul's Cathedral –

(**HANNAY** *swings on to the stage.*)

HANNAY. *WHAT ARE THE THIRTY-NINE STEPS?*

(**MEMORY** *freezes with shock.*)

MEMORY. – St Paul's Cathedral –

HANNAY. *I SAID WHAT ARE THE THIRTY-NINE STEPS!!?*

MEMORY. Thirty-Nine Steps sir? Thirty-Nine Steps?

(**MEMORY** *looks wildly between the* **PROFESSOR** *and* **HANNAY**.)

HANNAY. Yes Mr Memory! For the last time! *WHAT ARE THE THIRTY-NINE STEPS?*

MEMORY. The Thirty-Nine Steps is an organisation of spies. They collect information on behalf of the Secret Service of – Secret Service of – Secret –

(*Sound effects: Gunshot and audience panic.*)

(**MEMORY** *collapses. The* **PROFESSOR** *appears in the box with a smoking revolver.* **HANNAY** *points up at the* **PROFESSOR**.)

HANNAY. There! That's the man you want Detective Chief Inspector Detective Albright!!

PROFESSOR. Too late Hannay! You see this is not *your* story. This is *my* story! And I decide how it ends. You don't destroy me Hannay! And you don't get the girl!

(He swings the pistol at **PAMELA.***)*

HANNAY. Down Pamela! Get down!

PROFESSOR. No no no you don't Hannay! You lose the girl and you die of grief! That's how your story ends. You thought you found true love! Afraid not old sport! You never will you see. You will die as you lived, unloved, all alone in your dull little rented Portland Place flat! A lost man. Forever lost. Such a sad story. So sad, so terribly terribly sad! Goodbye my dear young lady. I'm so sorry it had to end like this. Who knows? You and I, we might have –

> *(He aims at* **PAMELA.** *She braces herself bravely. Suddenly* **HANNAY** *is in the box beside him.)*

HANNAY. Oh no you don't Professor!

> *(He grabs the* **PROFESSOR.** *They wrestle savagely in the box. Crash in and out of view.)*

> *(Sound effects: A gunshot. Audience scream.)*

> *(A* **DUMMY PROFESSOR** *appears. Topples out of the box into the audience.)*

> *(Sound effects: Audience panic.)*

MR MEMORY. *(Gasps from the floor.)* Don't panic! Don't panic ladies and gents!

> *(Calls into the pit.)*

Victor! Victor! Bring on the dancing girls!

MUSIC: ["DANCING GIRLS MUSIC"]*

---

* A license to produce THE 39 STEPS, ABRIDGED does not include a performance license for any third-party or copyrighted music. Licensees should create an original composition or use music in the public domain. For further information, please see Music Use Note on page 3.

London Palladium. Backstage. Night.

(HANNAY *and* PAMELA *run on with the* COMPERE. *They kneel beside* MEMORY.)

MEMORY. Just a scratch Bert. I'll be alright.

COMPERE. Course you will old chap.

HANNAY. Mr Memory? What was the top-secret formula you were taking out of the country?

MEMORY. Will it be alright me telling you sir?

HANNAY. It will Mr Memory.

MEMORY. It was a big job to learn it sir. The biggest job I ever had to tackle! Here goes. (*Fast and without a pause.*)

The first feature of the new engine is its greatly increased ratio of compression, represented by r minus one over r to the power of gamma and nine, sequenced to the power of xy forty-nine squared and duplicated notwithstanding by thirty-two point, seventy-one point and eighty-eight point recurring, aligned to eleven double governor valves flowing—

(*He slumps. They bow. He wakes.*)

radially in series – with concentric bladin comin out the diaphragms with longtitudinal pressure exerted on the turbine-shafts, counterbalanced by a twelve point nine grooved piston heads at an angle of point sixty-seven point five omicron recurrin. This device renders the engine completely – silent. Am I right sir?

HANNAY. Quite right old chap.

MEMORY. Thank you sir. I'm glad it's off my mind at last sir.

(*He dies.*)

(**HANNAY, PAMELA, COMPERE** *bow their heads.*)

(*Sound effects: Dancing girls fade/busy street.*)

Oxford Street, Outside Palladium. Night.

(HANNAY *and* PAMELA *enter.*)

HANNAY. Well –

PAMELA. Well – you're a free man anyway.

HANNAY. Right.

PAMELA. Saved the world too.

HANNAY. We both did that.

PAMELA. Not really.

HANNAY. You did actually. Anyway – better be – um – you know –

PAMELA. Of course.

HANNAY. D'you want to –

PAMELA. What?

HANNAY. Probably not.

PAMELA. No.

HANNAY. Got the decorators in and – you know.

PAMELA. Quite.

HANNAY. Right. Well. Bye.

PAMELA. Bye.

(*Lights fade.*)

Hannay's Apartment. London. Night.

(**HANNAY** *in his armchair. Pipe between his teeth.*)

HANNAY. So there we are. That's me I'm afraid. And the sad story of my life. Richard Hannay. Thirty-seven years old. Sound in wind and limb. Irreclaimable, irredeemable, unreformable –

(*The door opens.* **PAMELA** *appears.*)

PAMELA. Poor little orphan boy who never had a chance.

(*She puts her arms round him.*)

This is the man I want Inspector.

HANNAY. What's that drumming noise?

PAMELA. I think it's our hearts.

HANNAY. Quite noisy.

PAMELA. Yes.

(*A little Christmas tree rolls on.*)

Happy Christmas Richard Hannay.

HANNAY. Happy Christmas Pamela Edwards. Can I call you Schnozzle?

PAMELA. No.

HANNAY. Right. So shall we – um –

PAMELA. About time probably.

(*They kiss. The tree lights up.*)

(*Snow falls at the window.*)

MUSIC: ["HALLELUJAH CHORUS"] – *Handel*

The End

ABOUT THE AUTHOR

PATRICK BARLOW is probably best known for his role as Desmond "Olivier" Dingle the Artistic Director and Chief Executive. Together with John Ramm as Raymond Box, they are the renowned two-man National Theatre of Brent, which Patrick created in 1980. The NTOB has become something of a legend in British theatre, television and radio. Their abbreviated comedy epics include: *The Charge of the Light Brigade, Zulu!!, The Black Hole of Calcutta, Gôtterdämmerüng Wagner's Ring Cycle* (in an hour and a quarter), *Greatest Story Ever Told, Love Upon the Throne* (the Charles and Diana story) which was nominated for an Olivier Award, *The Messiah, The Wonder of Sex, Massive Landmarks of the Twentieth Century* for Channel 4 and their many acclaimed Radio series include: *The Arts and How They Was Done, All the World's a Globe, Iconic Icons, Giant Ladies That Changed The World, The First Man on the Moon* and *How They Done It* for BBC Radio 4. They have won two Sony Gold awards, a Premier Ondas Award for Best European Comedy and a New York Festival Gold Award for Best Comedy. Patrick's other screenwriting includes: *The Growing Pains of Adrian Mole, The True Story of Christopher Columbus, Queen of the East, Van Gogh* (Prix Futura, Silver Bear Berlin Film Festival), *Revolution!!* (Best Comedy Jerusalem Film Festival), the BAFTA-winning *Young Visiters* and *Why Didn't They Ask Evans?* for the Miss Marple series and ITV Other Stage Writing includes: *A Christmas Carol* (nominated for an Olivier Award) starring Jim Broadbent as Scrooge, an adaptation of Milton's *Comus* for the Sam Wanamaker Playhouse at Shakespeare's Globe, *Ben Hur – Tale of The Christ, The Six Wives and Reg* for Hampton Court. For Radio: *Joan Of Arc and How She Finally Became a Saint* starring Dawn French and *Starchild* for BBC Radio 4, Patrick's publications include: *Shakespeare – the Truth!* and *All The Worlds A Globe – from Lemur to Cosmonaut – An Inexhaustible History of the Whole World.* Patrick's Screen and Theatre acting credits include: *Shakespeare in Love, Notting Hill, The Diary of Bridget Jones, Nanny McPhee, Absolutely Fabulous, Jam & Jerusalem, Miranda, Is It Legal?, A Very English Scandal, Why Didn't They Ask Evans?* adapted by Hugh Laurie. *Loot, A Funny Thing Happened on the Way to the Forum and 'Toad'* in Alan Bennett's *Wind In the Willows.*

The 39 Steps was a hit show with 139 characters played by four actors. It has been performed in over 40 countries worldwide and ran for nine years at the Criterion Theatre in the West End. *The 39 Steps* won Patrick an Olivier Award for Best Comedy, a WhatsOnStage Award for Best New Comedy in the UK and

Helpmann and Molière Awards in Australia and France for Best Play. His Broadway adaptation co-won the Drama Desk Award for Unique Theatrical Experience and was nominated for four Tony Awards including for Best Play and won two Tony Awards for Best Sound Design and Best Lighting Design. In 2010 *The 39 Steps* held a record as the longest running Broadway play in seven years having played 771 performances.

When the show finally closed in The West End, the London run had recorded the fifth-highest number of performances of any West End play. During the course of its run our Producers, Edward Snape and Marilyn Eardley, claimed they got through "3,000 pairs of stockings, 530 maps of Scotland, 38 pairs of handcuffs and 16 suspender belts".

It's estimated that 3 million people have seen a version of *The 39 Steps* worldwide.